Snow

A NOVEL

Maxence Fermine

Translation by Chris Mulhern

ATRIA BOOKS

New York London Toronto Sydney Singapore

ATRIA BOOKS

1230 Avenue of the Americas
New York, NY 10020

Copyright © 1999 by Arléa

English Language Translation Copyright © 2001
by acorn book company

Originally published in France in 1999 by Arléa

This translation first published by acorn book company,
England, 2001

ISBN: 0-7434-5684-X

First Atria Books hardcover printing January 2003

10 9 8 7 6 5 4 3 2 1

ATRIA BOOKS is a trademark of Simon & Schuster, Inc.

For information regarding special discounts for bulk
purchases, please contact Simon & Schuster Special Sales
at 1-800-456-6798 or business@simonandschuster.com

Designed by Jaime Putorti

Printed in the U.S.A.

For Léa

Rien que du blanc à songer

ARTHUR RIMBAUD

1

Yuko Akita had two passions.
Haiku.
And snow.

A haiku is a Japanese poem. It has three lines. And only seventeen syllables. No more, no less.

Snow is a poem. A poem that falls from the clouds in delicate white flakes.

A poem that comes from the sky.

It has a name. A name of dazzling whiteness.

Snow.

2

Winter wind
—a monk, walking
in the wood

ISSA

Yuko's father was a Shinto monk. He lived on
the island of Hokkaido, in the north of Japan,
where the winter was long and hard. He had
taught his son the importance of faith, respect for
the power of the elements, and a love of nature.
He also taught him the art of writing haiku.

One day, in the month of April 1884, Yuko
reached his seventeenth birthday. In Kyushu, in
the south of Japan, the first cherry trees were
beginning to bloom. In the north, the sea was
still frozen.

His boyhood was nearing its end. The time
had come for him to choose a vocation. For gen-

erations now, the Akita family had either entered the religious life or the army. But Yuko had no desire for either.

On the morning of his birthday, Yuko and his father were walking along by the river, "Father," he said, "I want to become a poet."

The monk wrinkled his brow in a way that was barely perceptible and yet revealed a deep disappointment. The sun was reflected in the ripples of the water. A moon-fish glided past the birch trees and disappeared under the wooden bridge.

"Poetry is not a profession. It is a way of passing the time. Poems are like water. Like this river."

Yuko lowered his gaze to the quiet, flowing water. Then he turned towards his father and said:

"That is just what I want to do. To learn to watch the passing of time."

3

Frozen in the night
the water-jar cracks
wakes me

BASHÔ

"What is poetry?" asked the monk.

"It is a mystery," answered Yuko.

One morning, a water-jar cracks. A drop of poetry forms in the mind. Its beauty touches the soul. It is the moment of saying what cannot be said, of making a journey without taking a step. It is the moment of becoming a poet.

Do not break the silence. Just watch, and write. A few words. Seventeen syllables. A haiku.

One morning, something wakes us. It is time. Time to withdraw from the world. Time to look afresh at this life, passing.

4

The first cicada!
he said, and
pissed

ISSA

Months passed. In the summer of 1884, Yuko wrote seventy-seven haiku. Each as beautiful as the one before.

One morning of pale sun, a butterfly alighted on his shoulder and left a tracery of stars that the rain of June washed away.

Sometimes, during the hours of the siesta, he went to listen to the singing of the girls picking tea.

Another day he found the dried skin of a lizard in front of his door.

The rest of the time nothing happened.

When the first days of winter returned, the

time had come again to decide on Yuko's future. His father took him to the foot of the Japanese Alps, deep in the heart of Honshu province. He pointed out one of the peaks, its crest covered in eternal snow. He gave him a knapsack of food and a silk parchment, and said to him:

"Come back when you have made up your mind. Monk or warrior. It is for you to decide."

The boy climbed the mountain, heedless of the dangers it held and of his own tiredness. When he arrived at the top he found shelter beneath a rock. He sat down contemplating the splendor of the world.

He remained like this for seven days, sitting where the sky begins, marvelling at the beauty before him. On the silk parchment he wrote just one word, a word of dazzling whiteness.

When he returned, his father asked him:

"Yuko, have you found your way?"

The boy knelt down and said:

"I have found even more, father. I have found snow."

5

On this snow covered moor
if I die here, I, too will become
a Buddha of snow

CHÔSUI

Snow is a poem. A poem of a dazzling whiteness.

In January it covers the North of Japan.

There, where Yuko lived, snow was the poem of winter.

In the first days of January 1885, despite the wishes of his father, Yuko began his career as a poet. He wrote with only one purpose in mind. To celebrate the beauty of snow. He had found his way. And its beauty would never cease to enchant him.

9

In the days of snow he would leave the house in the early morning and begin walking toward the mountain. He always went to the same place to compose his poems. He sat down, legs crossed, beneath a tree. And he stayed like this for hours and hours, pondering in silence the seventeen most beautiful syllables in the world. Then, when finally he felt he had his poem, he would write it on silk paper.

Everyday a new poem, a new inspiration, a new sheet of silk. Everyday a different landscape, a different light. But always haiku and snow. Until nightfall.

Then he would return for the tea ceremony.

6

They play at rackets
innocent
their legs open wide

TAIGI

One evening Yuko did not return.

It was full moon. He could see as clearly as if it were the middle of the day. An army of clouds came to cover the sky. Ranks of white warriors conquering the sky.

It was the army of the snow. Yuko, sitting beneath the moon, silently watched their intrusion. He did not return until dawn.

On the road, in the pale freshness of the sun, he met a girl drawing water from the fountain. As she leant over, her tunic opened by her underarm to reveal a breast as white as the snow.

11

. . .

In his room a little later, Yuko touched his forehead: it was as hot as a cup of boiling sake.

He fell asleep, his penis, hard in his hand, like a red chili pepper.

Outside it was freezing.

7

So cold
the white petal
I bring to my lips

SÔSEKI

There are five things you can say about snow.
It is white.
It freezes nature and covers it.
It is always changing.
It is slippery.
It turns itself into water.

But Yuko's father had nothing good to say about snow. For him this strange passion his son had developed was making the winter seem even more hostile.

"It is white—so it is invisible. And does not deserve to exist.

13

"It freezes nature and covers it. Such arrogance, to turn a living thing into a statue of ice?

"It's always changing—well then, it can't be trusted.

"It's slippery—and who enjoys slipping over in the snow?

"It turns itself into water—true—and then it floods us during the thaw."

Yuko, on the other hand, saw five different characteristics. And each appealed to a different aspect of his artistic nature.

"It is white. Like a poem of great purity.

"It freezes nature and covers it. Making every landscape a painting.

"It is always changing. Like a piece of calligraphy. For there are ten thousand ways to shape the word snow.

"It is slippery. So it is a dance. For in the snow we all become dancers. Keeping our balance like tightrope walkers.

"It turns itself into water. Therefore it is music. For in the springtime it turns rivers and

14

streams into symphonies of white-flowing notes."

"So it is all of this to you?" asked the monk.
"And much more."
That night, Yuko's father realised that haiku alone would not be enough to fill the eyes of his son with the beauty of snow.

Yuko loved the art of haiku, snow, and the number seven.

Seven is a magic number.

It has both the balance of the square and the height of the triangle.

Yuko had started his career as a poet when he was seventeen.

He wrote poems of seventeen syllables.

He had seven cats.

He had promised his father to write only seventy-seven haiku each winter.

For the rest of the year he would stay at home, and forget about snow.

9

One day in the spring, when the sun had returned, a famous poet from the court of Meiji got to hear of Yuko's work. He went to the village where Yuko lived, and sent for Yuko's father. The monk, rushing back from the nearby temple, welcomed the distinguished courtier with great honor. He offered him tea, and said:

"Tonight my son will return from the mountain for the last time this year. Today is the day of his seventy-seventh haiku. But if you wish I can show you the study where he keeps his poems."

The poet breathed in the fragrance of the tea, and his heart was filled with joy as he remembered the occasion when he himself had been discovered by a master poet and brought before the Emperor. He smiled as he recalled the verse he had recited. A verse that had met with the Emperor's approval. Then he took a sip of the tea and said:

"Show me these wonders."

The monk led him into a room where the walls were covered in silk parchments. It was a scene of breathtaking beauty.

"There, Master. These are the haiku my son has written."

The poet advanced with great dignity. And read each of the seventy-six poems of snow that Yuko Akita had composed that season.

When he was finished, the monk saw that his eyelids were beaded with tears.

"Amazing. Your son is indeed a poet. Perhaps one day, when I myself have passed away, the Emperor will appoint him in my place."

Yuko's father, bursting with joy, threw himself at his feet.

"Nevertheless," added the poet, "I have to confess that there are two things that disturb me."

Startled, the monk lifted his gaze.

"Why?" he asked. "Are these not the most beautiful haiku since those of the great Bashô?"

"The work is surely without equal. The words are drawn from the very wellspring of beauty. They have a music all their own. But they have no color. Your son's writing is so desperately white. It is almost invisible. If your son wishes to present his work to the Emperor, he will first have to learn to bring color to his poems.

"But do not forget. He is very young. He is only seventeen. He will learn. And what else?" he asked.

The poet requested a second bowl of tea, and sat down on the veranda in front of the house, gazing at the mountain in the spring breeze. Then he drank another sip, and asked:

"Why snow?"

10

When Yuko came back from the mountain to discover that a stranger had read his poems and even worse had liked them, he flew into a rage.

"They are just attempts," he said. "I am still only learning my art."

"But they have already requested your presence at court!" said his father. "It is an honor, a great honor."

"No, father," said Yuko. "It would not be an honor. It would be a betrayal."

When he heard what the poet had said, Yuko became even more angry.

"And what does he know about painting and all its colors? There are ten thousand ways of painting, ten thousand ways to write a poem. But for me they all resemble snow. I will go to the

Emperor when I have written ten thousand syllables. Ten thousand syllables of a dazzling whiteness. Not one less."

"But ten thousand syllables will be almost . . . five hundred and ninety haiku! With seventy-seven poems each year that will take you . . . seven years!"

"Well, in that case, I shall go to the court in seven years' time."

And that was the last time either of them spoke of the visit of the Imperial Poet.

That spring, Yuko kept his promise and did not write a single poem.

He contented himself with breathing the scent of the cherry blossom in the green of the garden.

In the summer he breathed the aromas of wild honey, while the moon was bright, on the peaks of the mountains.

In the first days of rain he found a chanterelle, growing in the moss by the river.

It was a still and perfumed year.

11

*The skin of women
the skin they conceal
how warm it is!*

SUTEJO

The second winter of poetry was of a dazzling whiteness. It snowed even more than usual.

One winter's night, the girl from the fountain introduced him to the pleasures of love. Her skin was as sweet as the flesh of a peach. He took her breast in his mouth, suckling it like a moon-white lemon. And they stayed that way until dawn.

Yuko wrote seventy-seven haiku that winter, each one as white and as beautiful as the one before.

The last three he wrote were:

> Virgin snow
> a pathway of silence,
> and beauty

> The creak of snow
> in my footsteps
> —the cicada of winter

> Squatting woman
> pisses, and melts
> the snow

A haiku. A thing of clarity.

Spontaneous, familiar, and with a simple, subtle beauty.

To some people, perhaps, they said little. But for a poetic spirit they were ways toward the divine, ways to the white light of the angels.

12

In the first days of spring, the sun returned. And with it the Imperial Poet.

This time he was not alone.

With him, was a young woman of dazzling beauty. Her skin was pale and her hair was as black as the night. She, too, was a lover of poetry—the master's protégé.

Yuko's father welcomed them both with great reverence and offered them a rare and delicious tea. They sat outside on the veranda, beneath the flowers that hung down from the eaves.

As the master and the young woman sipped at the tea, Yuko's father said to them:

"My son feels unworthy of this honor. He says it will take him seven years to perfect his art, and until then, he is unfit to appear before the Emperor. This was only his second winter of poetry, so we will still have to wait another five years."

Before making his reply, the old poet stared at the river for a long time.

"Five years is a long time. I'm not sure that the Emperor will wait so long. When will your son return?"

"At nightfall."

"We will wait for him."

When Yuko returned from the mountain, he found the two visitors in his study. He fell immediately under the spell of the young woman, although the master's face inspired only indifference.

"Yuko," said the Imperial Poet, "I have two questions for you."

"I am listening, Master."

"Why seven years?"

"Because seven is a magic number."

Yuko noticed the briefest of smiles form on the lips of the young woman. Those lips reminded him of the freshness of a piece of fruit. He had to restrain himself from biting them.

"And why snow?" continued the master.

"Because it is poetry, calligraphy, painting, dance and music at the same time."

The old man drew closer to Yuko and asked him:

"So it is all of this to you?"

"And much more."

"You are a poet. But what do you know of the other arts? Do you know how to dance, or to paint, to write in calligraphy, or to compose music?"

Yuko did not know what to say. He could feel his face turning red.

"I am a poet. I write poems. This is the only art that matters to me."

"That is where you are wrong. For poetry is the music, the dance, the painting and the calligraphy of the soul. If you wish to become a master poet you will have to have the gift of the absolute artist. Your poems are marvellously beautiful, they flow, they have music. But they are white like the snow. You are not a painter, Yuko. Your poems have no color. And without it, they will remain invisible to the world."

The old man was beginning to irritate him.

But the young girl was beautiful. Very beautiful.

"Very well, Master," said Yuko. "I shall do as you say."

"In the south of Japan, there lives a man who has mastered all the arts. He writes poems, he composes music, but first, and foremost, he is a painter. His name is Soseki. He was my own master. Go and visit him, and he will teach you what you still have to learn."

The girl didn't say a word. She just stared at Yuko, smiling and taking long sips of the steaming tea.

"Do not waste a moment," said the poet, "because Soseki is very old, and his days are surely few."

Yuko bowed his head, and said:

"Master, I shall go and visit Soseki. I shall leave tomorrow."

Then he turned, and bowed awkwardly to the young woman. She let out a small mocking laugh, a laugh that hung in the air.

Yuko felt a surge of hatred, and at the same time an immense love for her.

13

That night, Yuko made love with the girl from the fountain. They lay in the snow, beneath the crystalline branches of a cherry tree. They made love seven times. Passionately. Till his sex was like a withered artichoke, and hers was like a purple crack.

14

The next day at dawn, Yuko left his village. He said goodbye to his family, and took the road heading south.

It was a journey toward the sun in his heart. The purity of the world and of its light were everywhere around him. As he went on his way, Yuko felt a pure and dazzling joy. He was free and he was happy. And all he had with him was his belief in love and in poetry.

But Yuko had grown to love snow so much, that he'd lost all fear of it. And that love almost killed him.

While he was crossing the Japanese Alps, Yuko was overtaken by a terrible snowstorm and lost his way. He found himself at the mercy of the elements. He took shelter beneath a rock which offered some protection from the wind and crouched there, on the point of exhaustion, numbed by the cold, alone in the dark and the snow, alone in his own silence. And there, where he could have died a hundred times of the cold, of hunger, of sheer exhaustion, there in the depth of his despair, he survived.

He survived because of what he saw that night, that vision from the other side of reality. The most beautiful thing he had ever seen. An image, he would never forget.

15

And what he saw was a woman. As he crouched beneath the overhanging rock, she was there, in front of his eyes. A young woman, naked and fair—a European. Asleep in the ice.

16

But she was not sleeping. She was dead. And her coffin was as clear as glass. Yuko immediately fell in love with the beautiful stranger.

Indeed to him, it wasn't like being near the body of a dead person at all. For hers was not a body. But a marvellous presence.

And then the questions began to form in his mind. What was she doing here, naked beneath the ice? And where was she from? And how long had she been here? And, come to think of it, did she even really exist?

The young woman trapped under the ice seemed as insubstantial as a dream. The pale-gold of her hair, the ice-blue of her eyes. And her face as white as the snow.

Yuko looked at her in silence, transfixed by her beauty.

17

For a while, Yuko thought he was dreaming.

For it seemed to him that the image of the young woman was allowing itself to be moulded and shaped by his thoughts. But what he saw was not a vision. She was actually there in front of him. And he was in love with her.

All night Yuko stayed there, filling his eyes with the image of the woman in the ice. And he never grew tired of looking at her, not even for a moment, but stayed there, motionless, despite the cold, contemplating a beauty he could never have imagined.

Time came to a standstill for him, that night. Who was this woman, and why was she here? That, he didn't know.

But of one thing he was certain, though he would grow old, and in time pass away, her face would never age. And even after he had gone, his love would be there forever.

18

At the first light of dawn, Yuko put a cross to mark the place where the young woman lay. Then he went upon his way.

He would never be able to forget what he had seen. The image of the young woman stayed with him for the rest of the journey.

That evening he arrived at a mountain village. He found himself in the middle of a square, and was so tired that he fell to the ground by the side of a frozen fountain. An old peasant brought him a cup of sake.

Yuko looked up at him, took a sip, and on regaining his breath, he asked:

"Who is she?"

And then collapsed in the arms of the old man.

19

It took seven days before he had regained his strength and was ready to resume his journey.

For those seven days, Yuko slept and dreamt about the woman of the snow. Then one morning, he got up, thanked the peasant for looking after him, and went on his way. He told no one about what he had seen.

20

He crossed the whole of Japan and one morning he arrived in front of Soseki's door. He was greeted by a servant whose name was Horoshi. An old man with a kind smile, hollow cheeks and grey-speckled hair.

"The poet of the Court of Meiji has sent me here," said Yuko, "to learn the art of color from master Soseki."

The servant stood to one side and Yuko entered a very cosy room, he sat down cross-legged on a mat, in front of a garden filled with hundreds of plants. He was given a bowl of steaming tea.

Outside, by the river, a bird was singing an enchanting melody.

"I come from very far away," said Yuko. "I am

a poet. More precisely I am the poet of the snow. I come here to follow the teaching of master Soseki."

Horoshi nodded.

"And how long do you wish to study with the master?"

"As long as it takes. I wish to become a complete poet."

"I see," he said. "But you must understand that my master is very old and tires easily. He has not long to live. That is why he teaches only the most gifted pupils. And only twice a day. In the morning at dawn and in the evening at dusk. Because of the light, naturally."

"Naturally. And if I am not worthy of his teaching, I will leave immediately."

"Master Soseki will be the judge of your ability. Here he comes now. It is time for his walk among the flowers. It is from them that he draws the intensity of his colors."

Horoshi pointed at a man who was advancing very slowly in the garden. Yuko turned to face the master and saw an old man with a long white beard; he was walking very solemnly, placing one foot precisely in front of the other, almost as if he was walking on a rope. He was smiling with happiness. His eyes were closed.

"And that is the master of color?" Yuko asked.

"Yes, it is he. The great painter Soseki."

"But he is . . . His eyes . . . "

"Yes," said Horoshi. "My master is blind."

21

How could a blind man teach him the art of color? The Poet of the Imperial Court had sent him all this way to learn the art from a man who could not even see his own work! Yuko was tempted to give up straight away, and go back to his beloved mountains. But Horoshi held him back.

"Do not leave so soon. Soseki may not be able to distinguish colors as clearly as he used to, but he sees with his soul what your eyes cannot see. Come, I will introduce you to him."

"But what can a blind man teach me about the intensity of colors?"

"As much as he can teach you about women. Although it has been a long time since he has shared a bed with one. Do not rely on appearances. For they will only confuse you."

Horoshi did not exactly introduce him, so much as push him in front of the master.

"Well," said Soseki. "Who are you? And what do you want from me?"

"I am Yuko, the poet of the snow. My poems are beautiful, but of a desolate whiteness. Master, teach me how to paint. Teach me about color."

Soseki smiled and answered:

"Very well, and you can teach me about snow."

22

The master's teaching method was certainly original.

On the first day, with the river still bathed in the soft light of the dawn, Soseki asked Yuko to close his eyes and imagine color.

"Color is not something outside us. It is within us. Only the light is outside," he said. "Tell me what you can see."

"Nothing. With my eyes shut I can only see black. Why, what do you see?"

"I can still see the blue of the frogs and the yellow of the sky," said Soseki. "So, which one of us is more blind?"

Yuko was about to point out that the sky is not yellow and frogs are not blue, but he refrained from making any comment. Perhaps the old man was crazy. Maybe he was going senile. In any case, he had no wish to contradict him.

"Master," he said, "I am beginning to see."

"What do you see?"

"I can see the red of the trees."

"Don't be foolish," said Soseki. "That's impossible. There aren't any trees here."

23

On the second morning, the master asked Yuko to close his eyes and said:

"The light is within us. Only color is outside. Close your eyes and tell me what you can see."

"Master," said Yuko, "I see the white light of the snow."

While saying these words, Yuko felt himself smiling. It was a nice spring morning. The sun was burning like an anvil.

"It is true," said Soseki, "it snowed here last winter. You are beginning to see."

24

So the master agreed to accept Yuko as his student.

And Horoshi, the servant, became his friend.

One night, Yuko asked him:

"Who is the master? And does he really know everything about art?"

"Soseki is the greatest artist in the whole of Japan. He knows about painting, music, poetry, calligraphy and dance. But his art would never have seen the light of day were it not for the love of a woman."

"A woman?" enquired Yuko.

"Yes, a woman. Because love is the most difficult of all the arts. And to write, or to dance, to compose, or to paint, these are the same thing as to love. It is like walking a high-wire. The most difficult thing is to keep going forward, without falling. And this is what happened to Soseki. Eventually he fell. Because of his love for a woman. And it was his art that saved him from despair and death. It is a long story. I don't think you'd find it very interesting."

"No," implored Yuko, "please tell me!"

"The story goes back to the time when the master was a samurai."

"Soseki? A samurai? Go on, I beg you!"

Horoshi took a sip of sake, and, faced with the young man's persistence, he allowed himself to drift back into his memories.

"Everything began by magic . . . "

11

25

Everything began by magic. One winter's day in 18. . . , Soseki was returning from battle. And it was then that he fell in love with a woman. A woman unlike any he had ever met.

In those days, my master was a samurai in the service of the Emperor.

He had taken part in a violent battle. A battle that had ended in a brilliant, and unexpected victory. He was coming back victorious. Wounded, but triumphant. He had received a deep wound in the shoulder, a sword-cut from an enemy warrior. Soseki could not get the scene out of his mind—the flavor of mud and of blood everywhere in his mouth, the enemy soldiers who threw themselves against him—and then that face, twisted with hate. The man was upon him, about to run him through. Soseki felt the chill of a blade on his forehead, then a roar of thunder as the canons fired. And then nothing. Nothing but a body without a head, a body that still twitched, and staggered and then fell on top of him. Its dead weight driving the blade deep into his shoulder. As if forcing upon him the horror of a battlefield that neither should ever have known. But that was how it was in those days. The days of chivalry. And such were the rewards of war. To die or to come back wounded. The samurai was never able to forget that vision of a man without a head. It was the most horrible thing he had ever seen in his life.

After the sword cut, he passed out. He lay there on the battlefield, everyone presumed he'd been killed. He lay there all night beneath that headless body. Eventually, next morning, someone finally heard his moans. They lifted the body to reveal Soseki's horrified face. They took care of him, but for several days the samurai continued to be delirious. Even after a week, there was still fear in his eyes.

The Emperor went to his bedside to congratulate him, and Soseki was proud of the honor, but his pride was still darkened by what he'd seen.

Eventually, when he had regained his strength, Soseki began the journey back to his village. He did not want to fight anymore, not because of the wound he had received—he had already been wounded six times since the start of the campaign—but from the pure disgust that he now felt for war. Having devoted his entire life to the army, he realised that he no longer had the desire to kill.

So he left the army and began walking home.

And it was on the way there that the miracle happened.

He was on the point of exhaustion, numbed by the cold, and with the horror of the war still fresh in his mind. He found himself alone in the depth of the darkness and the tragedy he had just lived through, alone in his own silence. And there, where he should have died a hundred times of cold, of hunger, of sheer exhaustion, he survived.

He survived because of what he saw that day, that vision that came from the other side of reality. A vision that came, no doubt, to balance the horror of the headless man. The most sublime, the most beautiful thing he had ever seen. An image he would never forget.

26

And what he saw was a woman. A young woman walking along a rope, high in the air above the silvery river. Her movements were graceful and flowing, and she seemed to be drifting through the air, as if by magic.

And to those who saw her from way down below, as she stood on the invisible rope with the balancing-pole in her hands, she looked like an angel.

Soseki slowly drew closer to the river, enchanted by her beauty. It was the first time he'd seen a European woman. And it seemed to him she was flying.

Entranced, he drew closer still. Until she was directly above him.

A crowd had gathered on the riverbank, drawn by this strange apparition.

Soseki approached an old man and, still looking up, asked him:

"Who is she?"

The old man, without even looking at him, answered with a tremor in his voice:

"She is a tightrope walker. Though she seems like a bird, somehow trapped in the air."

27

She was a tightrope walker, and her whole life followed a line. A line that led straight ahead.

28

She came from France. And her name was Snow. She had been given that name because she had very white skin, eyes blue as ice, and hair of pale gold. And also, because as she flickered in the air, she seemed as light as a snowflake.

This is how it began. One day, while Snow was still a young girl, she came across a traveling circus. It was a marvel to her. She felt she was dreaming, dreaming with her eyes wide open.

She knew straight away that this was the life for her, and decided there and then to become a tightrope walker. From that day she had gone on, step by step gradually raising the level of the wire, and perfecting her art. And so she became one of the first women to tread the high-wire.

She had set foot on the rope, and would never again come back down to earth.

29

Snow had become a tightrope walker for her love of balance. From that moment on, her life had unfolded the way a tangled rope unfolds, a rope woven from the turns of fate and the flatness of normal existence. Gradually, she mastered her art and overcame the constant danger of walking the high-wire.

She never felt so at ease as when she was walking on the rope a thousand feet up in the air. Her gaze straight ahead. Never wavering from her path.

For such was her destiny.

To go forward, step by step.

From one end of life to the other.

30

Snow had thrilled every square in Europe with her exploits. By the age of nineteen, she had covered many miles on her tightrope, and with every step she'd been risking her life.

She had tied her rope between the two towers of Nôtre Dame in Paris and had balanced there for hours, suspended above the Cathedral like an Esmeralda of wind and snow, and silence.

She had performed in all the great cities in Europe, each time defying the laws of balance. For she was no ordinary tightrope walker. But moved through the air as if by magic.

And looking up at her, from way down below, her body upright, like a white flame in the sky and her fair hair caressed by the wind, she seemed like the goddess of snow. And the truth was, that for her, the most difficult thing wasn't keeping her balance, or overcoming her fear, nor even walking on that endless rope. The most difficult thing as she moved through the light of the sky, was not to turn into a snowflake.

31

Her fame had led her all over the world. She had even crossed the Niagara Falls and the Colorado River. Then, almost without realising it, she arrived in Japan. It was the first time a foreign artist had performed in the country of the samurais. And a samurai was watching her, and he had already fallen in love.

For what he saw was poetry, painting, calligraphy, music and dance all at once. She was Snow and she was all that is beautiful in art.

When the beautiful stranger had reached the other side, and had finally come back to earth, Soseki could no longer hold back. He went toward her, and as he did so, he saw her delicate features, the shape of her mouth, the line of her eyebrows, and in that moment he realised that he would never again forget that face. He looked into her eyes, and she looked back into his. There was no need for words. She smiled, and in that smile Soseki lost his soul.

He knelt down, put his sword at his feet, and said:

"You are the one I have been looking for."

32

As it happened, Snow hadn't been looking for anyone. But Soseki's gesture was so beautiful that she was deeply moved. And she married him.

The first years were happy. The birth of their first child drew the couple even closer together. She was a girl. She had the ethereal beauty of her mother and the black hair of her father. They called her Spring Snowflake.

Theirs was a life of peace and silence. Snow gradually grew accustomed to life in Japan. Sometimes she missed her own country, but she never complained. For what she missed most was not her home, but her art. What she missed was the high-wire.

One night she dreamt she was flying. Next

morning, as soon as she woke up, she remembered her dream. But after that, she didn't think about it again.

Winter arrived. And then spring. The days lengthened, and the little girl began to grow up. Snow was happy. On the one hand she had the love of her husband, and in the other her own, which she gave to the child. And that fragile balance was enough to keep her on the thread of happiness.

33

But there came a day, when that fragile balance gave way. When the love between them was no longer enough to keep her happy. For she missed her life up there in the air. And she felt once again the longing for the height, the thrill and the sense of victory that came from walking the high-wire.

She asked Soseki to let her perform one last show. She wanted to walk a tightrope from one peak to the other, high in the Japanese Alps.

Her husband thought it was madness, seeing no sense in her putting her life at risk in this way. But like a true samurai, he bowed and gave his consent.

He ordered some steel rope to be sent over from Europe. Then he sent two servants to set the rope between the two highest peaks, in the centre of Honshu Province.

Snow laced up her ballet shoes, took her balancing pole from its case, and spent hours practising in their garden, walking back and forth along a rope, above the mountains of flowers and a miniature ocean on which yellow water-lilies were floating.

Soseki never tired of watching her. On the rope, his wife was a dancer without equal. And as he watched her walking, she looked so happy, so beautiful, so ethereal, that every day Soseki thanked the sky for having given her to him.

Her hair was fair. Her gaze was clear.

And she walked in the air.

34

The performance was set for the first days of summer. People came from all over the land to watch. It is said that even the Emperor himself was there, alongside the samurai.

As Snow put her foot on the rope, a murmur went up from the crowd. She was so high up, that she seemed just a small white speck in the air, a snowflake in the immensity of the sky.

With her balancing-pole in her hands, she went forward, step by step, gradually getting closer to the far side of the mountain. A minute passed, an hour passed. Down below, everyone held their breath. One false step, and death was certain.

But the young woman went forward. Step by step. Breath by breath. Silence by silence.

She never faltered.

35

The rope snapped. It came loose from the rock, sending the woman and the balancing-bar plunging downward. Those who saw her fall from afar, thought they had seen a bird falling from the sky.

Her body almost certainly fell into a crevasse, and was never found again. Snow had become snow and was sleeping now, in a bed of whiteness.

36

Soseki never recovered from the loss of his wife. The two servants who had tied the rope were dismissed straight away. A few days later it was discovered that they had died by throwing themselves from the side of a mountain. To Soseki, the news brought neither joy nor pain. He was aware only of his own suffering. He knew he would never again see the woman he loved. Never again see Snow. Never again behold such beauty.

Back home, his life now empty, he threw his old uniform away. His days as a samurai were over. He would never again be an officer of the Emperor.

Instead, he would devote himself to caring for

his daughter, and to art. To absolute art. For he could see the face of the woman he loved reflected in the face of the young girl, and she became for him the source of his inspiration. Through art he hoped to regain the balance that his wife's death had shattered. And so, for the love of a woman, he became both poet, musician, calligrapher, dancer. And painter.

And since painting was the most direct link between the face he loved and absolute art, and was also the surest way to find Snow again, it was in this art that the master excelled.

Soseki bought a wooden easel, silk brushes, a palette, and an infinite array of colors. He had a small shed built in the garden and there he locked himself away. He spent years painting the face of a woman he would never see again, except in his dreams.

But Soseki was never satisfied with his work.

Although his paintings were very fine, they seemed to him to be poor likenesses, for there was too much color in them. To paint a true portrait of Snow he would have had to paint a picture that was completely white. A painting without color.

But how could one paint such whiteness? The portraits of the young woman were all beautiful, but none of them resembled snow.

Soseki went on painting, day after day, night after night, never tiring in his quest for perfection.

But old age was creeping up on him. His little daughter had now grown up to be a beautiful woman, and he'd sent her to Tokyo to continue her studies. The old man found himself alone in front of the canvas, still contemplating the image of his lost wife. His eyes had grown tired from years of incessant work. And one day, his sight failed altogether.

It was on that very day that Soseki, in the depth of his blindness, painted the whitest and most beautiful of all his portraits.

III

37

"Well there you are," said Horoshi, "and that's how the story ends. My master never forgot his wife, just as he never stopped loving her, never stopped painting her. Not even when he become blind. In fact, especially since he became blind. For it was from the deepest darkness, that Soseki painted whiteness, and discovered purity. He discovered that true light and true colors are always intrinsically linked to the beauty of the soul. And so, beginning with the image of a woman who had disappeared, he has developed absolute art. Starting where there was no light at all, he has gone on to master light and all its shades. He has reached the very essence of all art. And that is why Soseki is a great artist."

The servant fell silent. Yuko gave a shiver. He looked at the old man and said:

"I know where this woman is. I came across her on my way here. She is dead, but it is as if she were still alive. She lies in a coffin of glass. She is so beautiful that I spent an entire night just looking at her."

As Yuko was speaking, his gaze had taken on a vague, distant look, as if his eyes were still veiled by the breath of a dream. The story had been long, and deeply moving. It was hard to return to the world of reality.

Horoshi just smiled at the young man, and nodded his head. But of course he didn't believe him for a moment.

38

The next day, as they sat by the bank of the river, Soseki asked Yuko to close his eyes and to imagine whiteness.

"Whiteness is not a color. It is an absence of color. Close your eyes and tell me what you see."

"Master, I see a coffin made of glass. And inside, I see the face of a woman. She is there in front of my eyes. A young woman, naked and fair, and as frail as a dream. She is dead. And she sleeps beneath the ice, deep in the mountains in Honshu province. Her name is Snow. And I know where she is."

At these words, Soseki's face froze. With his blind gaze fixed on the horizon, he said:

"But how could you possibly know these

things? Who are you anyway? A messenger from the shadows? No one knows where she is. The mountain took her a long time ago."

"No. The mountain that claimed her has given her back. Gradually, year by year, the army of the snow has recovered her body from the crevasse where she fell. She is there, beneath the ice, just below the surface. She lies in her coffin of glass, as beautiful now as when you last saw her. I promise you I know where she is. I saw her by chance while crossing the mountain. I was so struck by her beauty that I spent an entire night watching over her. I have put a cross on the site of her tomb of ice. And if you wish I will take you there."

The master then realised that Yuko was telling the truth, and he could not hold back a tear.

"I knew that one day she would send me a messenger. But I did not know he would arrive so late in my life."

Then he turned toward Yuko, and put a hand on the young man's shoulder.

"And to think that every day since she died, I have tried to recover the snow-like beauty of her face—through painting, and music, and poetry. And to think that her face is within reach of my gaze. And that I shall never see it."

39

The following day, when their lesson was over, Yuko asked Soseki:

"Have you thought about what I said? Shall I bring you to the place where your wife is buried?"

Soseki sighed, and said:

"My son. What would be the use of such a journey? I know that what you say is true, but it makes no sense for an old blind man to visit the tomb of a woman who died so many years ago. My wife is at peace now. And that peace should not be disturbed."

With that, he left Yuko and wandered off into his garden of flowers.

40

A month went by. Yuko did not mention the woman in the ice again. While for his part, Soseki appeared to have forgotten their conversation altogether.

Each day, the master greeted him before starting their lesson. And then made himself scarce for the rest of the day. At supper time he remained silent.

Then one morning, the old man turned to him and said:

"Yuko, only when you can bring together all that you know of painting, of music, calligraphy and dance, only then will you become a great poet. And there is another art also, an art that will teach you more than any of these—the art of the tightrope walker."

Yuko smiled. So the master had not forgotten.

"And why do I need to know about the art of tightrope walking?"

Soseki put his hand on the young man's shoulder, as he had done a month before.

"Why? Because to write, is to feel your way step by step along a thread of beauty. Along the thread of a poem, or of a story unfolding on a sheet of silk. For the poet, like the tightrope walker, must go forward, word by word, page after page, along the path of a book. And the most difficult thing is not that you must keep your footing on the rope of language, with only a pen for balance; nor to keep going straight ahead, when the way is blocked by the sudden drop of a comma, or the obstacle of a full stop. No, the difficulty for the poet is to stay on the rope that is writing, to live every moment without losing sight of his dream, and to never come down, not even for a second, from the rope of the imagination."

Yuko thanked the master for having taught him in such a subtle and beautiful way.

Soseki just smiled. And then he said:

"Tomorrow we shall go and find Snow."

41

They left at dawn. Yuko in front, and Soseki following the sound of his footsteps.

Each time they came to a place where the path was hazardous the young man offered his arm, but the old man refused. And each time he found his own way.

In the evenings, they slept as guests of the villagers, on mats rolled out on the floor. For whenever they arrived in a village no sooner had Soseki said his name than doors opened to them as if by magic. Everyone in Japan seemed to know who he was. Yuko was surprised. And realised then how fortunate he'd been to study under such a master.

42

The journey was long, and of a whiteness that had no end.

White as cherry blossom.

White as the silence that accompanied the steps of the two travelers.

Finally, one morning, the peaks of the first mountains appeared. Their path began to climb toward pure, clear sky.

This was the hardest part of the whole journey.

Soseki was beginning to show signs of tiredness. But Yuko pretended not to notice. For now they were close to the tomb of ice.

The journey was nearing its end.

43

When Yuko saw the cross, he felt his heart begin to quicken.

"Master!" he shouted, "I"ve found it!"

Yuko rushed up to the rock, to the place where he'd sheltered on the night of the storm. And he let out a cry of surprise.

"What's wrong?" asked Soseki anxiously. "Has she slipped forever into the heart of the mountain? Has there been an avalanche?"

"No," said Yuko. "Not at all. It's as if the army of the snow had known of our coming. Snow is here. But her body is even closer than before. She is so close to the surface I can almost touch her."

And there she was, beautiful, naked, and as frail as a dream. She was dead. But she seemed to be still alive. As if she were merely resting under the ice. And would soon be set free.

She wasn't naked, as he had first thought. Her costume had been under the ice so long as to become almost transparent. And her body seemed even more delicate and her skin even paler than before.

Yuko threw himself on his knees and began to scrape away the ice with his nails. At last, Snow appeared. Yuko took Soseki's hand and touched it gently to the young woman's face.

"Can you feel her face? Can you feel her skin?"

The old man caressed the cheek of his lost love.

Soseki was blind. But he did not need his eyes to recognise the contours of a face. And the slightest pressure of his hand on her eyelids was enough for him.

"It is really her," he said. "It is Snow. You were right."

He fell to his knees and the warm tears trickled down his face.

44

Soseki never returned from the mountain. He lay down on the ice, alongside his beloved, and closed his eyes.

Yuko tried to dissuade him, telling him that staying here was an act of madness. But the master answered him calmly:

"Leave me here, in peace. I have found my place. And here I shall lie, for all eternity."

Then he fell asleep, beside the body of the young woman.

And so he died, allowing himself to be overcome by the whiteness of the world.

He was happy.

He had reached the very summit of happiness.

45

Yuko came down from the mountain alone.
He went north.
Toward the snow.

He never looked back.
Never turned from the path.
As if walking a rope, from the south to the north of Japan.

46

When he finally arrived home, his father wanted to know all about his journey and about the teachings of the master. But Yuko did not answer. He locked himself in his study and did not reappear for several days.

One morning, unable to stand it any longer, the monk asked why he was shutting himself away.

"Father," Yuko answered, "Soseki has passed away. Now, please let me be, while I mourn him."

He locked himself in and began weeping.

But the truth was, that despite their friendship and the admiration he felt for him,

Yuko was not crying for the death of his master.

He was crying for his love, lost in the snow.

47

For many nights he dreamt about the woman in the ice.

About Snow.

One night the girl from the fountain knocked at his door and offered herself to him. But the young man turned her away, giving a tired sigh. The girl ran away in tears and Yuko never saw her again.

The seasons slipped away, like sand through an hourglass.

In the first days of winter, the snow began to fall. And the ink of the first poem began to darken the fibres of silk. Writing those first words, Yuko felt his heart becoming lighter. But it didn't last. For only poetry could hold back his pain. And as soon as he put down his pen, he could feel his heart become as cold as ice.

It was a long winter, a winter of dazzling whiteness.

48

But in the first days of spring, Yuko's writing changed. Little by little his poems began to take on color. Even he was surprised.

The teaching of master Soseki had finally started to bear fruit.

Yuko had become a master poet.

His haiku were no longer desperately white. They contained all the colors of the rainbow. His writing was clear, precise. And full of color.

But the land of his heart remained strangely covered with whiteness.

49

One April morning, a year after the death of Soseki, a young woman arrived at their house. The monk recognized her. She was the student of the Imperial Poet. The young woman for whom his son had felt both a tremendous hate, and an immense love. This time she was alone.

The monk received her with great reverence and offered her a bowl of steaming tea. She drank it slowly, looking at the river. Then he led the way into his son's study.

When she entered the room Yuko was carefully inscribing a haiku. As soon as he saw her, his pen slipped on the parchment and traced a strange mark. A straight line interrupted by a comma. Like a sketch of someone balancing, on a rope.

Yuko turned toward the young woman and smiled at her. Without saying a word, she came closer to him and laid a hand on his shoulder. Then she leaned over the work of the young master and said:

"This is without doubt the most beautiful portrait of my mother that has ever been painted."

The young woman's name was Spring Snowflake.

50

The young man looked at the drawing in front of him. And looked at her. And realised that it was the same dream come true, through that veil of reality that still lingered around him.

"I have been waiting for you for a long time," he said.

The young woman rested her head on his shoulder and closed her eyes.

"And I knew you would have waited even longer."

51

That night they made love for the first time. He, the young poet, and she, the daughter of his master, and of the woman of the ice.

As he entered her, she cried out so loudly that Yuko shuddered with emotion. He kissed her eyes, her breasts, her stomach.

In the morning, they let sleep overcome them.

Outside, it was snowing.

52

There are two kinds of people.

There are those who live, and who play, and who die.

And there are those who tread paths along the high crests of life. Balancing each step of the way.

There are the actors.
And there are the tightrope walkers.

53

Yuko never went to the court of the Emperor.

And Spring Snowflake never become a tightrope walker.

For there was no reason for history to repeat itself.

They were married on the first day of summer, on the bank of the silvery river.

54

And they loved each other
suspended on a thread
of snow.